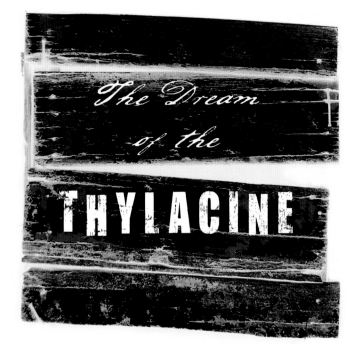

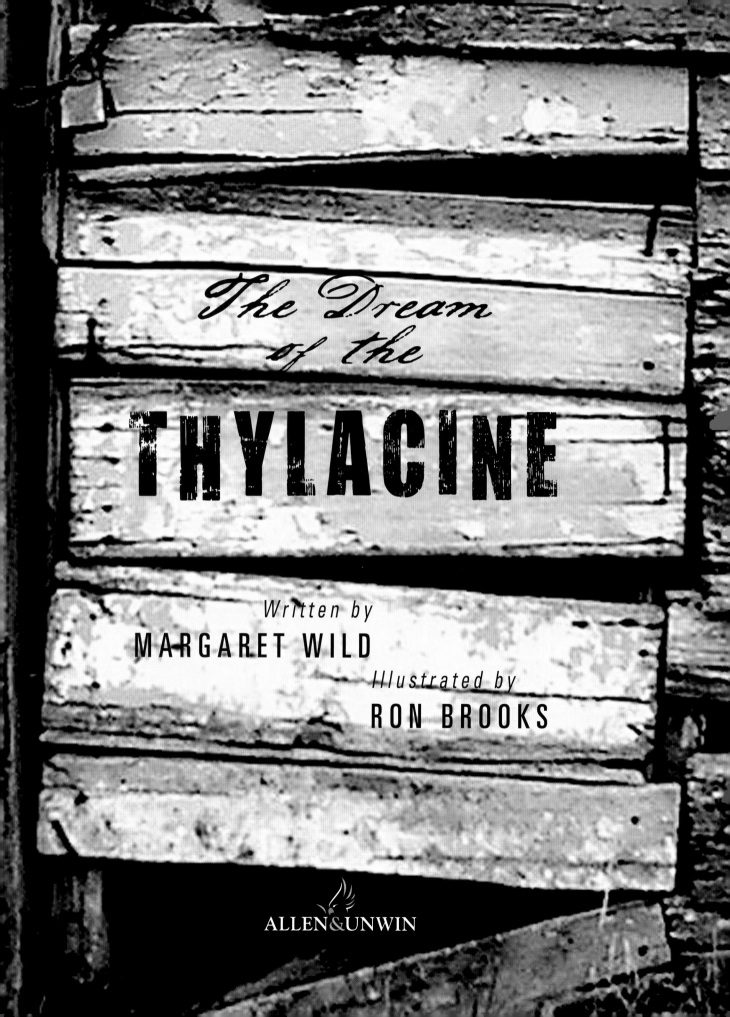

The Dream of the

THYLACINE

Written by
MARGARET WILD

Illustrated by
RON BROOKS

ALLEN&UNWIN

First published in 2011

Allen & Unwin
83 Alexander St
Crows Nest NSW 2065
Australia
Phone: (61 2) 8425 0100
Fax: (61 2) 9906 2218
Email: info@allenandunwin.com
Web: www.allenandunwin.com

A Cataloguing-in-Publication entry is available
from the National Library of Australia
www.trove.nla.gov.au

ISBN 978 174237 383 6

Ron Brooks used acrylic on board and mixed media for the artwork in this book.
Designed by Ron Brooks
With special thanks to Yvonne Burger and Sandra Nobes, for helping me put it all together.
This book was printed in September 2012 at South China Printing Co. Ltd., Daning Administrative District,
Humen Town, Dongguan City, Guangdong Province, China.

10 9 8 7 6 5 4 3

Teachers' notes available from www.allenandunwin.com

Trapped am I,
in cage of **twisty** wire, **cold** concrete.

PROWL
RAGE
HOWL

Know you not that I am tooth and claw –
see me hunt through bracken and bush,
        see me swagger across wild lands,

        see me glory at the edge of cliff.

Ailing am I,
in cage of **twisty** wire, **cold** concrete.

MOURN

Ache

YEARN

Know you not that my heart is a forest –
run with me through trees of striply bark,
run with me over creeks of flickering fish,

run with me where the snow falls slow.

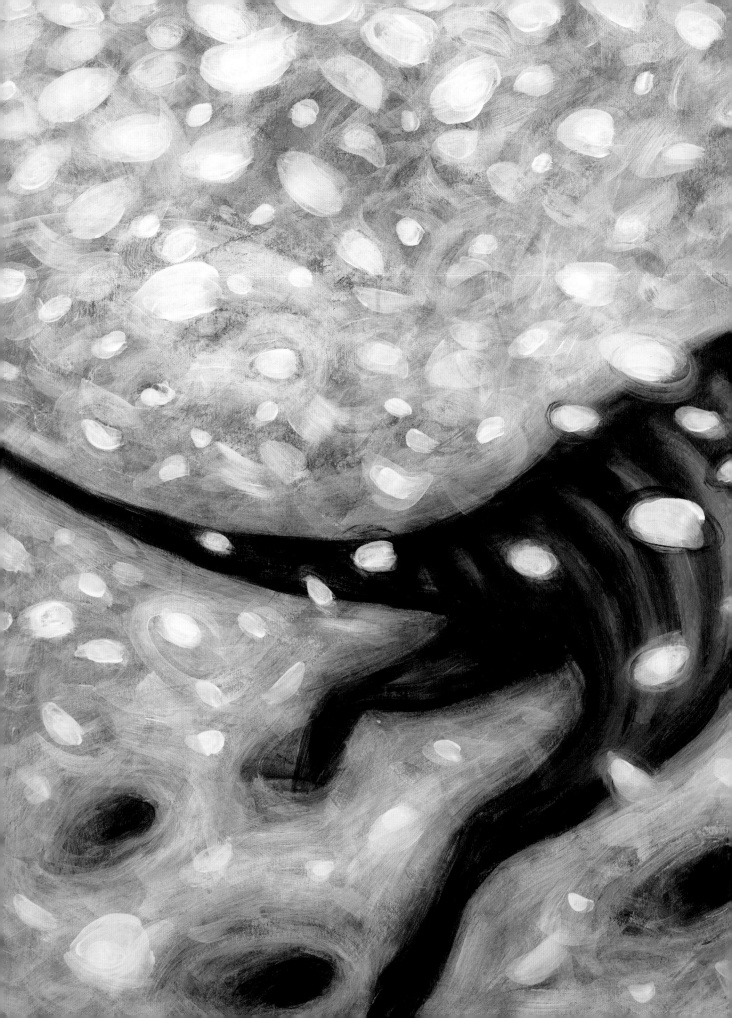

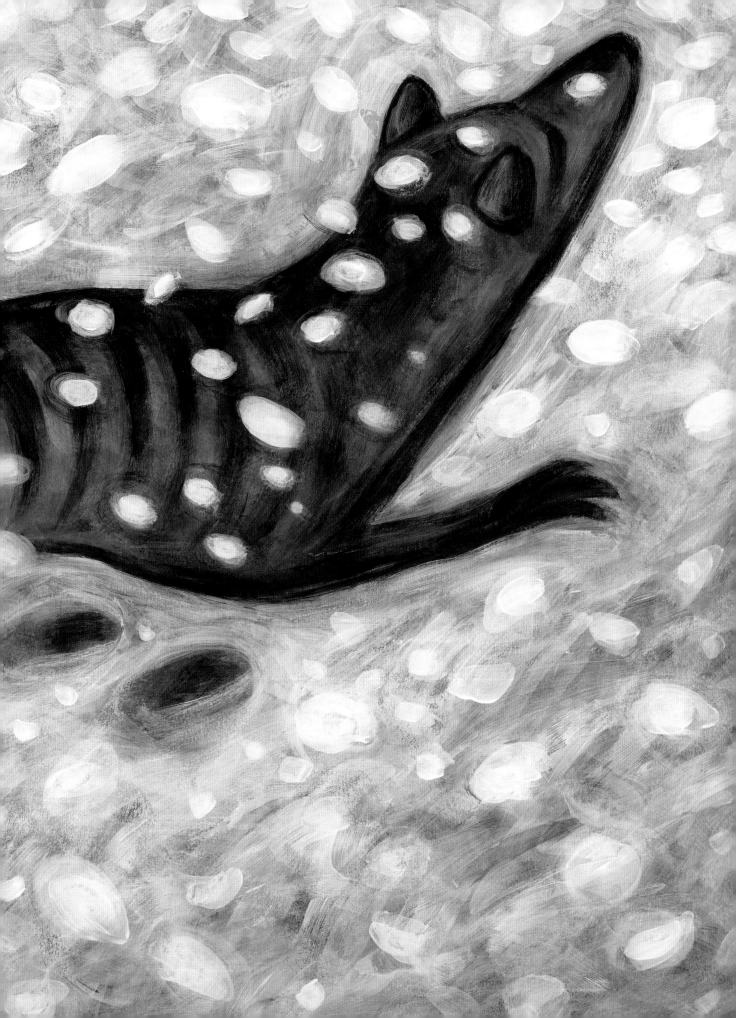

Shadow am I,
in cage of twisty wire, cold concrete.

Thin
STILL

Mute

Know they not that my spirit flies free –

seeking the mouth of the river,
the arms of the mountains.

Rest now.
Hear the stones chant,
the wind console.

Dreaming am I.

The Thylacine, also known as the Tasmanian Tiger,
was a large carnivorous marsupial now believed to be extinct.
Though people do hold out some hope that this unique creature
might indeed still be out there in the Tasmanian wilderness,
the sad truth is that this is very unlikely.

The photographic stills in this book are taken from the
1937 BBC film of the last confirmed surviving Thylacine,
which died in the Hobart Zoo in the late 1930s.

MARGARET WILD has written many remarkable books, including the novels *Jinx* and *One Night*, and the picture books *First Day*, *Ruby Roars*, *Woolvs in the Sitee*, *Lucy Goosey* and *Puffling*.

RON BROOKS is acclaimed as the maker of many well-loved picture books, including *The Bunyip of Berkeley's Creek*, *John Brown, Rose and the Midnight Cat*, *Motor Bill and the Lovely Caroline*, *Henry's Bed* and *Henry's Bath*. His memoir on book-making is *Drawn from the Heart*.

As well as *The Dream of the Thylacine*, they have created three other exceptional picture books together: *Old Pig*, *Rosie and Tortoise* and *Fox*.